Pluto's Best

A LEVEL PRE-1 EARLY READER

By Susan Ring

Illustrated by Loter, Inc.

DISNEP PRESS

New York

An Imprint of Disney Book Group

Meeska, Mooska, Mickey Mouse!

Let's go into my .

Clubhouse

is going to be in a contest.

Pluto

 is going to be in it, too.

Butch

They both want to win the big .

prize

Oh, Toodles!

Here are today's Mousketools:

five yellow , a , and a .

balls   life preserver   whistle

Goofy begins the contest.

Oh, no!  only has one ●.
ball

Pluto
He needs to juggle six ●●●.
balls

Oh, Toodles!

Do you see a tool that could help Pluto?

Yes! can use the five yellow ●●.
Pluto   balls

wins!

Pluto

He gets a big blue .

star

 and  run and jump.

Pluto   Butch

Oh, no! Pluto, come back!

 can't hear us.

Pluto

Oh, Toodles!

Which tool can we use to call  ?

Pluto

Cheers! We'll use the

 .

whistle

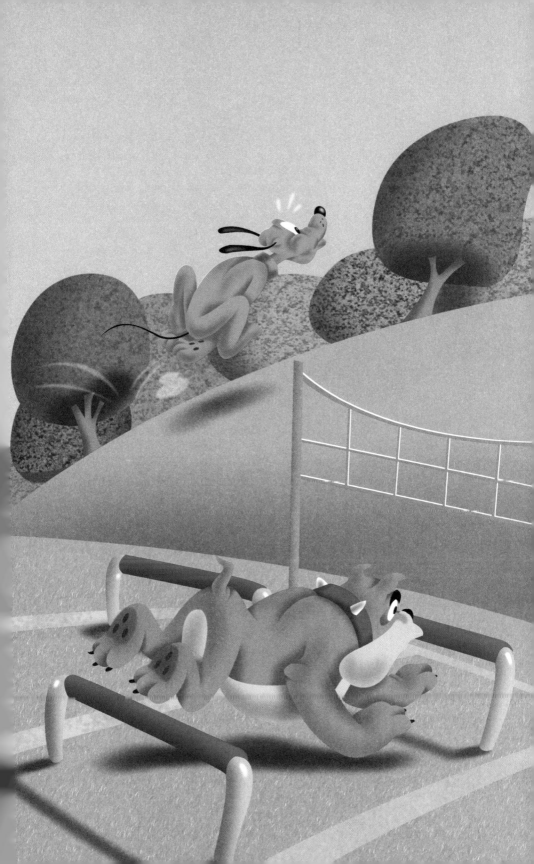

 Butch wins!

He gets a big red  star .

 Butch wins the next game—wagon pulling.

He has two stars.

How many does Pluto have?

Now it is time to swim.

Who will get to the end of the pool first?

Oh, no!  needs help.
Butch

Oh, Toodles!

Will the  help save Butch?
life preserver

Yes!

Go,  , go!
Pluto

You can help  .
Butch

 helps  get to the end!
Pluto   Butch

 wins!
Butch

He gets a big red  .
star

He gives it to  .
Pluto

Now  and have the same number

Butch   Pluto

of stars.

stars

Let's count them!

Yes, they have two stars each.

stars

They both share the big prize!

prize